Help! A
Vampire's Coming!

Help! A Vampire's Coming!

by ABBY KLEIN

illustrated by

JOHN MCKINLEY

THE BLUE SKY PRESS
An Imprint of Scholastic Inc. • New York

To Toes and Schmoopie—
May you always have sweet dreams. . . .
I love you!
—Mooka, a.k.a. Mama

THE BLUE SKY PRESS

Text copyright © 2005 by Abby Klein
Illustrations copyright © 2005 by John McKinley
All rights reserved.

Special thanks to Robert Martin Staenberg.

Library of Congress catalog card number: 2004020763
ISBN 0-439-55606-6
10 9 8 7 6 5 4 3 2 1   05 06 07 08 09
Printed in the United States of America   40
First printing, September 2005

CHAPTERS

I have a problem.

A really, really, big problem.

I keep having these nightmares

about a vampire.

Let me tell you about it.

CHAPTER 1

Go to Sleep!

"Freddy," my mom called. "Turn off the TV. It's time for bed. Tomorrow's a school day!"

"Just five more minutes. PUULEEEAASE, Mom. This *Commander Upchuck* is my favorite one."

"No! Now!" my mom said. "Turn that TV off right this minute, and go brush your teeth. It's getting late."

"Can I have a glass of water?"

"I said go brush your teeth."

"But I'm really thirsty."

"Oh all right, but do it quickly."

I got myself a drink, and then I went into the bathroom to brush my teeth. I'm old enough now to brush my teeth all by myself. I even have my very own toothpaste, bubblegum flavor with blue sparkles.

I love to look at myself in the mirror and sing while I brush. "Freefrre, Freefrre, Bo Freefrre, Baraaara, Franna, Fro, Freefrre, Meeee, Mii, Mo, Mrefree, Freefrre."

"Freddy, are you finished yet?" my mom called as she came down the hall.

"Arllmosss!"

Just then my mom came into the bathroom. "Freddy, spit already. It's time for bed."

"PHHEWWW!" Half of the toothpaste sprayed all over the mirror.

"Freddy! Please watch where you spit!"

my mom yelled. "Look what you just did to the mirror! What a mess!"

"I'll clean it up for ya, Mom."

"No, I'll clean it up later. It's time for bed. Get in your room, *now*!"

"OK, OK, I'm going."

I got into bed, and my mom read me a story from a fairy-tale book my grandpa got me for Christmas. It's really cool. It's got knights and big dragons. And I love when the knight cuts the dragon's head off.

My mom finished reading. "OK, sleepy-head, snuggle up." She pulled up my shark blanket, tucked me in, and gave me a kiss. "Sweet dreams. See you in the morning."

"'Night, Mom. I love you."

My mom turned out the light and closed the door.

"MOM!" I yelled.

She opened the door. "What?"

"Dad forgot to kiss me good night."

"I'll go get him. You stay in bed."

My dad came in and gave me a big bear hug and a wet, sloppy kiss. "Good night, Mouse. Sleep tight."

"Good night, Dad. I love you."

My dad closed the door and started back down the hall.

"DAD!"

He opened the door. "What?"

"I need to go to the bathroom."

"Why didn't you go when you brushed your teeth?"

"I forgot."

"Well, make it snappy, Mouse. You need to go to bed."

I walked to the bathroom, but the door was locked. My sister, Suzie, was in there. She was always in there for no good reason, staring at herself in the mirror, thinking she was sooo beautiful! I banged on the door. "Hey, Poophead, open the door!"

"Why should I, Booger Breath?"

"Because I need to go pee."

"Go use Mom and Dad's bathroom."

"Suzie!" my dad called. "What are you doing in there?"

"Brushing my hair!"

"Well, open the door. Your brother has to go pee."

"Oh, all right. But I don't see why the baby couldn't use your bathroom," she said, opening the door.

"Suuu-zie," my dad said, "I've told you before not to call your brother a baby."

I stuck my tongue out at her as I squeezed past to get to the toilet.

"Dad! Freddy stuck his tongue out at me!"

"All right, enough, you two. Freddy, let's go. It's way past your bedtime."

I finished peeing and then climbed back into my bed. My dad tucked me in and closed the door.

"Dad."

He opened the door. "NOW WHAT?"

"You forgot to kiss me."

"I already kissed you."

"Not this time."

"Freddy, I will give you one more kiss, but this is it. Now GO . . . TO . . . SLEEP!"

He kissed me, turned out the light, and closed the door.

I stared up at my ceiling. I didn't want to shut my eyes because whenever I shut my eyes . . . THEY CAME. These ugly, horrible, yucky nightmares. I couldn't get them out of my head, and they were really, really scary—but I didn't want to tell anyone because then my sister would think I was a baby. My heart started beating really fast.

"MOM! DAD!" I yelled.

I waited, but there was no answer. So I tri[e] again. This time, I yelled a little louder. "MOM! DAD! I need you!" But still no one came. So I got out of bed and went into the TV room. I tiptoed in, snuck up from behind, and tapped my mom on the shoulder.

"AAAHHH!" she screamed. "Oh, Freddy, it's you. You scared me. I didn't know you were here."

"Uh, Mom, I'm thirsty. Can I have a glass of water?"

"You just had one right before bed."

"Well, I'm reaaally thirsty. PLEEEAAASE."

"If I give you a sip of water, then you have to promise me you'll stay in bed."

"OK. I promise."

My mom got me some water. "Just a sip. I don't want you to have an accident."

couple sips, and then my mom
e back in. "Good night, Freddy,"
, kind of grouchy, and closed the
do I really didn't want her to go. I didn't
want to be left in the room by myself.

"Mom?"

She opened the door. "WHAT?!!"

"What can I dream about?"

"I don't know . . . ummm . . . how about school tomorrow?"

"No, I don't want to dream about that."

"Playing basketball with Robbie."

"Nah."

"Your trip to the beach."

"Not that *again*!"

"Well, I'm not going to make a million suggestions. It's way past your bedtime, and you have school tomorrow. And *IF* you get out of this bed one more time, then you will be punished. Do you understand me?"

"What if I have to go to the bathroom in the middle of the night? Can I get out of bed then?"

"Yes," my mom said, letting out a big sigh. "Of course you can get up in the night to pee. But there is no reason for you to get out of this bed right now. Just go to sleep!" She turned in a huff, marched across the room, and slammed the door. I listened until her footsteps disappeared down the hall.

And I was left alone in the room.

Just me and the nightmares.

And I had no idea how to get rid of them. No idea at all.

I rolled over and grabbed my three favorite stuffed animals: Chompers the Shark, Eddie the dog, and Bananas the monkey. I squeezed them tight. "Well, guys, I think this is going to be a long night," I whispered. "I am going to keep my eyes open because if I keep them open, I can't have any nightmares, so I'll just

have to stay up all night. You guys can keep me company."

I lay my head back on my pillow and stared up at the ceiling as my heart thumped loudly in my chest. *THUMP, THUMP, THUMP!*

CHAPTER 2

Exhausted

I was up for most of the night because whenever I started to fall asleep, the nightmares came, and I had to open my eyes to make them go away.

The next morning when my alarm went off, I was so surprised I fell out of bed and hit the floor hard. UUGGGHHH!

"Freddy," my mom called. "Come on down. Time for breakfast."

I climbed back into bed. Just five more minutes. I could close my eyes now because it was the morning. The nightmares didn't come when the sun was out.

I must have fallen back asleep because the next thing I knew, Suzie was standing over me, yelling in my ear, "Get up, Brat! Mom says you'd better be at breakfast in five minutes, or else we'll be late for the bus! And I'm not waiting for you."

I stumbled out of bed, put on my clothes, and dragged myself down the stairs to the kitchen.

"Well, look who's here," said my mom. "Sleeping Beauty."

"More like one of the ugly stepsisters," Suzie said, laughing. "Looks like someone's having a bad hair day!"

"Leave him alone," said my dad from behind his newspaper.

I yawned loudly. "OOHHAAAWWW."

"You see, Freddy," said my mom, "this is what happens when you don't get enough sleep. You have to go to bed earlier."

I was so tired I could barely keep my head up. As my mom talked, my head nodded forward and snapped back, nodded forward and snapped back. Then, the next thing I knew, my face fell, *plop*, right into my cereal bowl. I could barely see through the oatmeal stuck to my eyelashes.

"Ha, ha, ha . . . look at Freddy. That is the funniest thing I've ever seen!" Suzie screamed with laughter.

"Freddy!" my mom yelled as she ran over and pulled my head out of the bowl. My

face was covered in mushy, wet oatmeal. "Are you all right?"

"Yeah, fine," I said. A lump of oatmeal slowly dripped off my hair and plopped onto the floor.

My mom cleaned me up and gave me another bowl of oatmeal. "Well, that does it, Freddy. There will be no *Commander Upchuck* for you tonight. You are going to bed early, and that's final."

"But, Mommm," I started to plead, as she cut me off.

"No 'buts.' You are exhausted. Just look at you. How do you expect to stay awake in school?"

"I could always stay home from school today, Mom."

"That's not fair!" Suzie complained.

"Suzie, be quiet," said my mom. "Besides,

I never said Freddy was staying home, so I don't know what you're whining about. Freddy, you are going to school. Being tired is not a reason to stay home. You'll just have to get more sleep tonight."

"Easy for her to say," I mumbled to myself. "She doesn't have nightmares."

"Well, I've gotta go," said Suzie as she grabbed her backpack and headed for the door. "I don't want to be late for the bus."

"Wait for your brother," my dad called after her.

"Yeah, wait for me!" I yelled. I grabbed my backpack with the shark fin on the back and ran to the door, but Suzie stopped me and said, "Where do you think you're going, Dog Breath?"

"To the bus."

"Like that?" she said, laughing.

"Like what?"

"In your underwear!"

"Huh?" I looked down. All I had on was my T-shirt, underwear, and socks. No pants. No shoes.

"I'm sure your little girlfriend Jessie would love to see your great white shark undies. They're so cute."

"She's not my girlfriend," I said. I tried to cover myself up with my hands. "I just forgot my pants."

"Well, you'd better go put some on, because the bus will be here any minute, and I'm not waiting."

I ran upstairs, threw on some pants and shoes, and raced back down just as the bus pulled up in front.

As I ran to get on, I tripped and scraped my knee on the sidewalk.

When I finally got on the bus, I leaned back in the seat and closed my eyes, hoping to take a quick nap on the way to school.

CHAPTER 3

Your Worst Nightmare

The next thing I knew, I felt a sharp pain in my side. It was my sister. She was poking me in the ribs with her elbow. "Hey, wake up, Ding-Dong. We're at school."

"Huh? What?" I sat up and rubbed my eyes. "What time is it?"

"Time to get off the bus, Bozo. And, uh, you might want to wipe that drool off your chin." She laughed as she ran off to class.

I wiped my chin with my shirt and slowly got off the bus. I had to squint because the sun seemed really bright, and I was still half asleep.

I dragged myself to Room 3. By the time I got there, the bell must have already rung because most of the kids had put away their backpacks and were already sitting on the rug.

I put away my stuff and sat down on the rug next to my best friend, Robbie. Mrs. Wushy was taking attendance. "Max."

"Here."

"Jessie."

"Here."

"Robbie."

"Here."

"Freddy."

Silence.

"I know Freddy's here. I saw him come in," said Mrs. Wushy.

"Hey," Robbie whispered, "she's calling your name."

"Oh, uh, here," I said, yawning.

"Man, you look awful," Robbie said. "What's wrong?"

"I really didn't sleep that good last night." I yawned again.

Mrs. Wushy finished taking attendance and then started giving directions for our morning work. "First, you need to cut out the . . . blah . . . blah . . . blah . . . "

I just couldn't concentrate. My eyelids were heavy, and my brain was all fuzzy.

"Freddy! Freddy," Robbie whispered as he poked me. "Mrs. Wushy's asking you a question."

"Huh? Uh, yes, Mrs. Wushy?"

"Freddy, please tell the kids what you do after you cut out all the pieces."

"Uh . . . um . . . uh . . . I don't know."

"Well, you need to pay more attention when I'm giving directions. Who can tell Freddy what to do next?"

"I can! I can!" said Chloe, waving her hand wildly in the air.

"Teacher's pet," I mumbled sleepily under my breath.

Mrs. Wushy finished explaining how to

arrange the cut pieces, and then we all went to our seats to start working. I had to hold my head up with one hand, so the other hand had to do all of the work. It's pretty hard to cut one-handed.

"Why are you so tired?" Robbie asked.

"I can't sleep. I keep having these really scary nightmares. Like a huge, ugly vampire is chasing me. I can't get away. He grabs me and sucks out all my blood!" My heart started beating fast just from telling the story.

"Cool," Max said and laughed. He's the biggest bully in the whole first grade. "I can't believe you think that's scary. You're such a baby."

"No, he's not," said Jessie. "I was having really scary vampire nightmares, too. They

were sucking my blood and then cutting me up into little pieces and gobbling me up! It was freaky."

"Stop it this instant," said Chloe, stamping her foot. "Don't say things like that. You're scaring me," she said, covering her ears.

"Well, I'm not scared anymore," said Jessie, "because my *abuela* told me that vampires don't like garlic."

"So?" I said.

"So, silly, I put garlic in my room to make them stay away."

"And it really works?"

"Yeah," said Jessie. "I haven't had any more vampire nightmares."

"Wow! Thanks, Jessie. I know what I'm gonna do right after school."

That is if I can stay awake until then.

CHAPTER 4

The Secret Mission

Robbie was coming over to my house after school to play, so I figured we could both go on a secret spy mission to get the garlic. We made our plans on the bus ride home.

As soon as the bus dropped us off, we ran into the house, and I bumped right into my mom. She was coming down the stairs.

"Hey, what's the rush?"

"Sorry, Mom. I didn't see you there."

"And where did this sudden burst of energy come from? This morning you were so exhausted you fell into your oatmeal."

"He did?" Robbie said, covering his mouth and trying not to laugh.

I glared at him. "It wasn't that funny."

"It really *was* funny," my mom said, chuckling. "Oh, Robbie, if only you could

have seen him with oatmeal smushed all over his face."

Now Robbie was really cracking up. "I'm sorry I missed it!"

"Thanks for sharing that, Mom. Well, we've got a lot of homework to do, so we'll see ya later," I said. I grabbed Robbie and started running upstairs.

"Wait!" my mom yelled. "Don't you two want a snack?"

"Uh, no, thanks! Like I said, we've got a lot of work to do."

"You're *sure* you don't want a snack?"

"No, no, that's OK. We'll let you know if we need you."

"Well, OK. I'll be in my office making some phone calls."

"Perfect," I thought. That will give us

time to sneak down to the kitchen and look around for the garlic. My dad was at work, Suzie was at her dance class, and once my mom got on the phone, she could talk for hours. She'd never hear us.

We dashed to my room, dropped our stuff on the floor, and went over our plans for the secret garlic mission. We would have to be really, really quiet. If we got caught, I would be in big trouble because according to my mom, the only room in the whole house where you are allowed to have food is in the kitchen. No "ifs," "ands," or "buts." No breakfast in bed. No snacks in front of the TV. Nothing. I remember one time Suzie snuck a piece of cake into her room. My mom found out, and Suzie got in BIG trouble. She couldn't watch TV for a week!

We took off our shoes because the kitchen floor was sparkly clean, and our shoes might leave footprints. My mom is like a detective that way. She always knows when someone has walked across her clean floor. We didn't want to leave any clues behind for her to find.

"Hey, do you have a black sweatshirt and some sunglasses?" Robbie asked.

"Why?"

"Because the really cool guys in spy movies always wear sunglasses and dress in black, so I thought it'd be cool if we did, too."

We got sunglasses and black sweatshirts, and then I went to my closet and pulled out this new tool belt my dad gave me for my last birthday. It has real tools, not plastic baby ones. There is a hammer, nails, a wrench, and a flashlight. You never know what you might need on a secret mission, so I hooked it around my waist.

"Hey, what about me?" said Robbie. "Don't I need tools, too?"

"Just this," I said, handing him a walkie-talkie. "You're going to be my lookout. You'll stand outside the kitchen, and if you see my mom coming, you'll say, 'Code red, code red.'"

I opened my door just a crack and peeked out. There was no one in sight. "Are you ready, Robbie?"

"Don't call me Robbie. Call me Agent X."

"OK. Are you ready, Agent X?"

"Yes, boss."

We slipped out the door and closed it behind us, so my mom would think we were still in there, working. We could hear her voice down the hall talking on the

phone. "Blah, blah, blah . . . " It was now or never.

We tiptoed down the stairs and into the kitchen without making a sound.

"OK, you go hide outside the kitchen door. Don't forget: If you see my mom coming, you radio me, and say, 'Code red, code red.'"

"Yes, boss."

Robbie slipped out the door, and I started snooping around.

Now the only problem was this: I had no idea what garlic looked like. I knew my mom used it to cook, and I knew what it tasted like, but I had never actually *seen* it. I started opening and closing all the cupboards, being careful not to let them slam shut, but no luck. I opened the fridge and looked inside. Nothing I didn't recognize.

"Any luck yet?" Robbie radioed in.

"Not yet. Is the coast still clear?"

"Yep. No enemy agent in sight."

"Huh?"

"No, your mom's not coming."

"By the way, do you know what garlic looks like?"

"Yeah, it's powdery. My mom shakes it on stuff."

"Great. Thanks. Over and out."

I decided to check the spice rack.

BINGO! There it was! Right next to the ginger. Garlic powder.

"Code red! Code red!" Robbie's voice crackled over the walkie-talkie.

I quickly took the jar and shoved it under my sweatshirt, closed the cupboard, and started walking out of the kitchen.

"AAHHHH!" I bumped right into my mother just as Robbie appeared from around the corner.

"What are you boys doing?" she asked.

My heart was beating a hundred miles an hour. "Oh, just getting a snack," I said.

"I thought you said you weren't hungry."

"All that work made us hungry."

"What did you have?"

"Just some string cheese. Well, we've gotta go finish. See ya later, Mom," I called as we ran upstairs and disappeared down the hall. I slammed my bedroom door shut and pulled the garlic out from under my sweatshirt.

"How is this stuff supposed to scare away vampires?" I asked Robbie.

"They don't like the smell," he said.

I opened the lid and took a deep sniff. "P.U., no kidding. This stuff stinks," I said, holding my nose. I closed the garlic powder and hid it in my dresser. I couldn't sprinkle it around now because my parents would smell it when they tucked me in tonight. I would have to wait until everyone was asleep.

"Whew, that was a close one," I said, slapping Robbie on the back. "Thanks, pal."

"You mean Agent X."

"Thanks, Agent X."

"Anytime. That's what friends are for."

CHAPTER 5

Vampires, Beware!

"Good night, Mom. Good night, Dad."

"Good night, Freddy. Now remember—no getting out of bed tonight."

"I won't."

"Are you sure you don't need a sip of water?" my mom asked.

"I'm sure."

"You're sure you don't need to go pee?"

asked my dad. "Because we mean it. No getting out of bed."

"No, I'm OK."

"Well, then, sleep tight. Sweet dreams," they said as they kissed me.

"Oh, they'll be sweet," I whispered to myself as they started to walk out.

My parents shut the door and left me alone in the dark.

I wasn't scared. I couldn't *wait* to go to sleep tonight. I had garlic powder. No vampire would get near me now!

I waited until it was really dark and everyone in the house was asleep, and then I went into action.

I opened the drawer where I had hidden the garlic powder, pulled the jar out, and twisted off the lid.

"P.U.!" I said, pinching my nose. "This stuff really does stink!" I started searching my room for my sharkhead flashlight.

Yeeowww! I smashed my pinkie toe on the corner of my dresser. I let out a silent scream and started hopping madly around my room, holding my throbbing toe and whispering, "Oww, oww, oww!"

I found the flashlight in my plastic Halloween pumpkin and shined it around the room. "Where do you guys think I should sprinkle the garlic?" I asked Chompers, Eddie, and Bananas.

"Next to the window," said Chompers.

"By the door," said Bananas.

"Under the bed," said Eddie.

"Thanks, guys. I hope I have enough to put some in all those places."

I tiptoed around my room and sprinkled garlic powder under the bed, on the windowsill, and by the door.

"There, that should do the trick," I said as I gave the jar one last, gigantic shake to make sure I had used every last bit.

I climbed into bed and hugged Chompers, Eddie, and Bananas. "Sweet dreams, guys," I whispered.

"Ewwww," they all said. "It really stinks in here!"

"Sorry, guys. It's supposed to stink. That's what keeps the vampires away. I know! Wait a minute."

I jumped out of bed, grabbed three clothespins out of my treasure box, and put one on each of their noses.

"I cadt breeed too gud," said Chompers.

"Me needr," said Bananas.

"Jut breed thru your mowt," said Eddie.

I was so tired I couldn't wait to get to sleep. "You guys don't need to keep me company tonight. I'm gonna sleep like a baby. Good night."

I let out a big sigh and closed my eyes. There I was, playing ball at the park. The sun was shining. The kids were laughing.

"Hey." I opened my eyes. "It's working."

I closed my eyes again and saw the park. Someone called my name. I smiled and turned to look and THEN . . . I . . . SAW . . . IT!!! A vampire! He was running after me. . . . He grabbed me. . . .

"AHHHH!" I sat up in bed and opened my eyes before he could suck my blood. My heart was pounding. I grabbed Chompers, Eddie, and Bananas and shook them. "Wake up! Wake up!"

"Hey, be careful. Yur gonna mate me frow up," said Bananas.

"Yeah, I'll tod my cookiesth all ober da bed," Eddie whined.

"Sorry, guys, but it looks like it's going to be a long night after all."

CHAPTER 6

That Plan Stinks

Riiinnnnggg. Riiinnnnggg. Riiinnnnggg.

I grabbed my alarm clock and threw it across the room. It crashed into my dresser and fell on the floor. I opened one eye and peeked at it. At least it stopped ringing.

As I started to fall back asleep, my dad came into my room and started shaking me. "Let's go, Mouse. Time to get up. Wakey, wakey, eggs and bakey."

"Five more minutes," I said, yawning.

I had just fallen asleep when the sun came up.

My dad sniffed the air: *Sniff, sniff. Sniff, sniff.* Then he started coming toward me.

Oh no! The garlic powder. I was so tired, I had forgotten all about it! I grabbed the jar and hid it under my pillow.

Then my dad leaned over and started sniffing *me*. "Freddy, I thought I told you to take a bath last night."

"I did, Dad."

"Well, something sure stinks in here."

"I don't smell anything," I said, sniffing the air.

"Then you've got something wrong with your smeller, because it really stinks!" My dad plugged his nose. "I can't stay in here anymore. Hurry up and get dressed, or you'll be late for the bus."

"Whew, that was a close one," I whispered to Chompers, Eddie, and Bananas.

I hurried to get ready for school because I didn't want my mom to come into my room next.

That day at recess I went over to play dodgeball. I really love dodgeball! I am like the dodgeball champion! I'm always one of the last kids left inside the circle.

But today I was so tired I could barely move. I saw the ball coming right at me, but my feet felt as if they weighed about one hundred pounds.

Doink. The ball hit me right in the chest and bounced off my nose.

"Ha-ha! What a spaz! You're out, Spaghettihead!" yelled Max.

I went over to the bench and plopped my butt down.

"Freddy, please be careful," said Chloe. "This is a brand-new dress, and my mom doesn't want it to get wrinkled."

"Sorry, Fancy-pants," I said and yawned.

"Wow! You must really be tired," said Jessie. "You never get out."

"I *am* really tired."

"But I thought you were going to try the garlic."

"I did. It didn't work."

"It didn't?"

"Nope."

"That's weird. It worked for me. How many pieces of garlic did you use?"

"Pieces? I used garlic powder."

"Powder?" said Max, laughing. "You are so stupid."

"Ohhh no," said Jessie.

"What?"

"It only works with garlic *pieces*."

"How do you know?"

"I told you. My *abuela* told me, and she knows everything."

"Well, no more garlic for me. It stinks!"

"I have a dreamcatcher," said Chloe, "and it doesn't stink."

"A what?"

"A dreamcatcher. It's handmade by Native Americans, and they use it to keep bad dreams away. I hang it on the wall above my bed, and it catches all my bad dreams, so they can't get in my head."

"Where can I get one?"

"I don't know," Chloe said, shrugging her shoulders. "My aunt went to visit the Ojibway Reservation in Minnesota and brought it back for me."

"Great. That does me a lot of good."

"Why don't you lock your window?" said Robbie. "My dad locks my windows every night."

That just seemed too easy. I reached over and hugged Robbie. "You're a genius!" I said. "What would I do without you?"

CHAPTER 7

Lock 'em Up!

I couldn't wait to get home and test the lock on my window.

"Hey, Mom! I'm home!" I yelled as I dashed up the stairs.

"Freddy, is that you?" she called from her office.

"Yeah, I'll be in my room."

"OK. I'll be up in a bit. I just need to make a few more phone calls."

I threw open my door, dumped my back-pack on my bed, and ran to the window to check the lock.

Just my luck. It was rusty and loose. And definitely not strong enough to keep that vampire out.

I plopped down on my bed and stared at the ceiling. I hit my forehead with the palm of my hand and mumbled, "Think, think, think."

I turned toward my dresser, and that's when something shiny caught my eye.

"That's it!" I jumped up and grabbed my tool belt. "I can't believe I didn't think of this before."

Nails! Nails were better than a lock any old day. I could just nail my window shut. The vampire would never get through that!

I didn't want my mom to hear the

pounding, so I turned my CD player on real loud.

Then I hooked my tool belt around my waist and got to work.

Bang, bang, bang! Bang, bang, bang! I must've hammered in about forty nails.

I wanted to make sure there were no cracks where a vampire could slip through.

"There. That ought to do it," I said proudly. "Let's see you try to get through that, you stupid vampire."

CHAPTER 8

Scratch, Scratch

That night I whistled a little tune as I put on my pajamas. I smiled real big. Those vampires would never get me now!

There was a knock on my door. I jumped. "Freddy, are you ready for your bedtime story?" It was just my dad.

"Yeah, Dad."

"What should we read?"

"Can you read me one of the stories from my fairy-tale book?"

"How about 'Dracula's Castle'?"

"Nah. How 'bout the one with the knights and dragons?"

My dad found the book and started reading. "Once upon a time . . . "

Scratch, scratch.

"There was a horrible dragon . . . "

Scratch, scratch.

"Do you hear that?" my dad asked.

"Hear what?" I said.

Scratch, scratch.

"There it is again. It sounds like something is scratching at your window."

My heart started beating real fast: *THUMP, THUMP, THUMP!*

I heard it, but I didn't want my dad to go near the window, so I said, "I don't hear anything, Dad."

But this time the noise got louder. *SCRATCH, SCRATCH.*

"What on Earth . . . ?" my dad said. He got up and started walking toward the window.

"NNNOOOO!" I screamed as I leaped off the bed, trying to land on my dad's back and tackle him to the floor before he could reach the window.

Womph! I missed and landed face-first on the floor.

My dad pulled up the shade to look outside, and that's when he saw the tree branch that had been hitting my window. But he also saw the nails . . . all forty of them.

And boy, was he mad! His eyes popped out, and his face was bright red.

"FREDDY ALAN THRESHER!" he screamed. "WHAT DID YOU DO?"

I looked up from the floor where I had landed. "Don't be mad, Dad." I sniffled as a tear rolled down my cheek.

Just then Suzie and my mom came running into my room.

"Oh boy . . . you're in *BIG* trouble now!" Suzie said.

My mom just stood there with her mouth hanging open. Then she turned to my father. "I told you not to get him that tool belt for his birthday. He's too little."

"FREDDY, I WANT AN ANSWER THIS MINUTE. WHY IN THE WORLD WOULD YOU DO SOMETHING LIKE THIS?"

I started sobbing. "The vampires . . . blood . . . the window . . . chasing me . . . Jessie said garlic . . . stinky . . . no locks . . . THEY'RE GONNA GET ME!!!"

"What?"

"Freddy, come here," my mom said. She stretched out her arms toward me.

I got up and sat down next to her on the bed, and she hugged me tight. "I think I know what this is all about. Honey, are you having nightmares?"

"Yes," I said and sniffled.

"Well, why didn't you tell us?"

"I didn't want you to think I was a baby."

"We would never think that."

"You know . . . " my dad said. He had calmed down now, and his face wasn't so red. "Suzie used to have nightmares, too, when she was your age."

"Really?" I said, looking up at Suzie.

"Uh, no!"

"Suuu-zie," said my dad.

"Well, maybe a little." She nodded.

"Well, then, how did you make them go away?"

"Should we tell him our secret?" Dad asked, turning to Suzie.

"Yeah, let's tell him the secret. It looks like he needs them," said Suzie.

"Needs what?" I asked.

"Them," they answered together. "The Dream Police."

"The who?"

"The Dream Police."

"Who are *they*?"

"Well, you see, when Suzie was your age, she had really, really bad nightmares, too, so we called the Dream Police, and they've been protecting her room ever since."

"Cool!" I said excitedly. "What do the Dream Police do?"

"Well," said Suzie, "when you go to sleep, they stay up all night and are on the lookout for nightmares. If they see one, they shoot it with their toilet-plunger shooter, tie it up with their huge, gigantic, nightmare-catching net, and then spray it with their special vanishing spray and vaporize it."

"We can talk more in the morning," my dad said. "But right now I want you to get some sleep."

"Thanks, guys. I feel much better."

"Good night. Sweet dreams," they all said and left the room.

I snuggled under my covers, closed my eyes, and thought, "OK, Dream Police, do your stuff."

CHAPTER 9

Liars!

"Freddy," my mom called. "Let's go. Time to get up!"

I heard her calling me, but I was so exhausted I couldn't even lift my head off the pillow.

"Stupid Dream Police," I mumbled. "That's all a big, fat lie!" I think they all just made up that story to get me to go to sleep. Last night the vampire came again, and the Dream Police did not come to rescue me!

"Freddy!" I heard my mom calling again. "Get down here now, or you're going to miss the bus!"

I rolled out of bed, threw on some clothes, and stumbled into the kitchen.

"What happened to you?" Suzie asked, snickering. "You're a mess!"

I looked down at myself. I was wearing two different colored socks, my shirt was on backwards, and I had forgotten to put on my pants.

"For your information, I didn't get any sleep last night. Why? Because there are no Dream Police. I know you just made that whole thing up so I would go to sleep. They're not real. I called them last night, but they didn't come. They don't exist!"

"Now wait a minute, Freddy. Calm down," said my dad.

"Of course they didn't come," said Suzie. "They haven't been trained yet."

"Trained?"

"Yeah," said Suzie. "They don't just appear. You have to decide who you want your Dream Police to be, and then you have to train them."

"Who are *your* Dream Police?"

"Snuggles, Sweetpea, and Smiley. Chompers, Eddie, and Bananas can be yours. If you want, I can help you train them after school."

I ran over to Suzie and threw my arms around her. "You are the best sister ever."

"Yeah, yeah, I know. Now go change. I can't be seen with you like that!"

CHAPTER 10

Dream Police
to the Rescue

Suzie and I spent the afternoon training Chompers, Eddie, and Bananas how to be Dream Police.

That night I couldn't wait to go to bed. I knew those guys were going to vaporize that vampire's butt!

My dad came to tuck me in. "So, are Chompers, Eddie, and Bananas ready to report for duty?"

"Yep." I smiled. "That vampire is going to be sorry he ever came near this room! Good night, Dad."

"Good night, Mouse. Sweet dreams," said my dad, kissing my cheek.

"Oh, they'll be sweet. Good night."

My dad closed the door, and I heard his footsteps disappear down the hall.

I turned to Chompers, Eddie, and Bananas. "Are you guys ready?"

"Yes, sir, Captain, sir," they all said together and saluted.

"Let's kick some vampire butt!"

I snuggled under the covers, closed my eyes, and let out a big sigh. Finally I would get a good night's sleep.

As I started to drift off, the vampire appeared and started to come toward me.

"Get him, guys!" I yelled.

Chompers, Eddie, and Bananas leaped up. "Dream Police to the rescue!"

Chompers grabbed his toilet-plunger shooter and pulled the trigger. The toilet plunger flew across the room and pinned the vampire to the wall.

"Great shot," I said.

"You won't get away now!" cried Eddie as he ran over and threw the nightmare-catching net over the vampire's head.

The vampire struggled to get free, but he was tangled in the net.

"Say 'bye-bye,' you big, bloodsucking bully," said Bananas. "You're about to get vaporized." He aimed the special vanishing spray right in the vampire's face and squirted.

The vampire vanished into thin air.

I jumped out of bed, ran over to Chompers, Eddie, and Bananas, and I gave them all a huge hug. "You guys were awesome tonight!"

"Piece of cake," said Chompers.

"That was fun!" said Eddie.

"Get some sleep, Freddy," said Bananas.

"We've got ya covered."

"Thanks, guys."

I slept like a baby the rest of the night. When my alarm rang, I jumped out of bed, grabbed Chompers, Eddie, and Bananas, and I squeezed them tight. "You guys are the best."

"No problem," they said. "Now can we get some sleep? We've been up all night."

"Oh yeah, sure. Get all the rest you need. Then be ready to report for duty at eight o'clock sharp tonight."

I threw on my school clothes and raced downstairs.

"Well, it looks like someone got a good night's sleep," my mom said.

"Yeah," I said and sighed. "I had the best dreams. I hit a home run. I got a puppy. I went to Wacky World. Thanks, Dad."

"Now that you're no longer afraid of the dark, maybe we can try that camp-out in the backyard sometime soon."

"One thing at a time, Dad. One thing at a time."

DEAR READER,

I have been a teacher for many years, and I have two kids of my own. I know many children who are afraid of the dark, and I know how scary nightmares can be.

When I was little, I used to sleep with the covers pulled up over my head. I thought there was a monster living under my bed who would come out at night. My mom and dad made me some monster spray, and I used to spray it around my room every night to keep the monster from coming out.

I bet you've had some crazy nightmares. I'd love to hear about them. Just write to me at:

Ready, Freddy! Fun Stuff
c/o Scholastic Inc.
P.O. Box 711
New York, NY 10013-0711

I hope you have as much fun reading *Help! A Vampire's Coming!* as I had writing it.

HAPPY READING!

Abby Klein

Freddy's Fun Pages

FREDDY'S SHARK JOURNAL

I bet many animals that live in the ocean have nightmares about the great white shark. They are really scary!

THE GREAT WHITE SHARK

The great white shark can grow to be more than 21 feet in length.

It can weigh more than 7,000 pounds.

It has 2 to 3 rows of teeth, and when one falls out, another replaces it.

But don't worry, they don't *like* to eat people! In fact, they are afraid of us. Humans are their only enemy.

FREDDY'S DREAMCATCHER

At school, Chloe told me about her
dreamcatcher from the Ojibway tribe.
The Ojibway make dreamcatchers
to trap bad dreams and let the good
dreams flow into their minds.
When I was having bad dreams
I decided to try making a
dreamcatcher of my own.

To make a dreamcatcher like mine, you will need:
A small hoop or a plain, twig wreath from a craft
   supply store
A piece of yarn (or string) about five feet long
Some beads with large holes
A few feathers

1. Tie a piece of yarn
about two or three feet
long to one side of
the hoop.

2. Wrap the yarn around the hoop in a crisscross fashion to make a web-like design. When you run out of yarn, tie the other end to the hoop.

3. Cut another two or three pieces of yarn about six inches long, and string the beads onto them. Tie a feather or two onto the end of the pieces.

4. Tie these beaded strings onto the bottom of the hoop. Take another piece of yarn and tie it to the top of your dreamcatcher to make a loop. Hang it above your bed.

Sweet dreams!

MONSTER SPRAY

If you are having bad dreams or find yourself worrying about vampires, monsters, or other scary things at night, try making some of my special Monster Spray.

1. Get an empty spray bottle (the pump kind—you can find one at a drug store).

2. Fill the bottle with water.

3. Add two drops of perfume or lemon juice.

4. Cover the bottle with white paper and label it "Monster Spray." You can draw pictures all over the bottle of things that make you happy.

5. Spray a little bit in your room every night before you go to bed to get rid of the monsters. Monsters do not like happy pictures, or sweet or lemony smells, so they will stay away.

FREDDY'S TIPS FOR PREVENTING NIGHTMARES

1. Don't watch scary movies or read scary stories right before you go to bed.

2. Think about something fun that happened during the day when you lie down to go to sleep.

3. Leave your door open a little bit.

4. Use a night-light.

5. You can always sleep with your favorite stuffed animal or special blanket to protect you!

6. Squirt your monster spray.

Remember—nightmares are not real.
Just because you dream it,
it doesn't mean that it will ever
happen to you in real life.

Have you read all about Freddy?

Freddy will do anything to lose a tooth fast—even if it means getting in trouble with Mom!

Now that Freddy's found the best show-and-tell ever, how will he sneak his secret into school?

It's report time again, and Freddy's nocturnal research turns up some unexpected results!

Can Freddy beat out Max the bully to get the one open spot on the hockey team?

Help! Does anyone have a magic spell for talent?

Don't miss Freddy's next adventure! Coming soon!